Austin Dobson, George William Kohlmetz

Bibliographical Notes on a Collection of Editions of the Book

Known as Puckle's Club

Austin Dobson, George William Kohlmetz

Bibliographical Notes on a Collection of Editions of the Book Known as Puckle's Club

ISBN/EAN: 9783337222208

Printed in Europe, USA, Canada, Australia, Japan

Cover: Foto ©Raphael Reischuk / pixelio.de

More available books at **www.hansebooks.com**

BIBLIOGRAPHICAL NOTES

ON A COLLECTION OF EDITIONS
OF THE BOOK KNOWN AS

"PUCKLE'S CLUB"

FROM THE LIBRARY OF A MEMBER OF
THE ROWFANT CLUB
AS SHOWN AT THE CLUB HOUSE, MARCH, 1896

WITH AN INTRODUCTION BY
AUSTIN DOBSON

CLEVELAND
THE ROWFANT CLUB
1899

TO THE MEMBERS OF THE ROWFANT CLUB.

IN the fascinating but still-to-be-written *Romance of Bibliography*, there could be no more curious chapter than the story of Puckle's *Club*. That a book, meritorious, indeed, in its intention, but without sufficient distinction to secure a permanent place in the annals of English Literature, should be published in the same year as the *Spectator*, and should run through seven editions before the middle of the century, is perhaps not in itself unexampled. But that, after its decease in the last century, it should have been revived again early in this as an illustrated volume which forms an important link in the history of the revival of wood-engraving, is certainly a notable thing. It is, however, more notable still that a something both in the work and the author should continue to attract the attention of the book-lover. For several years Mr. G. Steinman Steinman, of Croydon, devoted much patient investigation to Puckle's biography, the results of which he embodied in 1872 in a privately printed and very rare tract of twenty pages entitled "The Author of 'The

Club' Identified"; and Mr. George W. Kohlmetz, of Cleveland, Ohio, has rendered no less signal service to the literature of the subject by bringing together a collection of editions of the book, which it may be affirmed, without fear of contradiction, has certainly no rival in England or America. It is curious to think what Puckle would have said if he could have foreseen this unexpected survival of the little manual of ethics which he revised and re-revised so carefully. Dr. Johnson, we are told, was highly gratified to hear that *Rasselas* had been reprinted in America. "The impression," he wrote in 1773, "is not magnificent, but it flatters an authour, because the printer seems to have expected that it would be scattered among the people." Yet the *magnum opus* of Puckle was not only reprinted in America, (Philadelphia, 1795,) but more than a century later it has received even greater honours. The Rowfant Club has made it the subject of a bibliography which is at once exhaustive and elaborate.

One result of the sustained interest in the book is that, at the present moment, we know, if not all we can know about the author, certainly a great deal more than has been known hitherto. At the beginning of the century, the editor of the reprint of 1817—presumably the Mr. Edward Walmsley who selected the work for illustration—was obliged to confess that he could find no material for a Memoir of the writer, and even the all-embracing Allibone, as late as 1875, could only supply an imperfect list of works. We are certainly better informed now. Thanks to Mr. Steinman and *Notes and Queries*, we are able to assert definitely that James Puckle was a Notary Public, and a partner in the firm of "Puckle and Jenkins" "in Pope's-Head-Alley over against the Royal Exchange"; that he was the author of two pamphlets, *England's Interest*, 1696, and *England's Way to Wealth and Honour*, 1699; that, in 1720, he obtained letters patent for the invention of a piece of quick-firing ordnance known as "Puckle's Machine," which, although much satirised among other South Sea projects, was tried successfully in 1722 to the admiration of all beholders; that he was a twice-married man with a family; and that, finally, he died in July, 1724, not long after the issue of the fourth edition of *The Club*, and was buried in the burial-ground of St. Stephen's, Coleman Street, one of the churches rebuilt by Wren after the Great Fire. This is not much. But considering that James Puckle was obscurely gathered to his fathers one hundred and seventy-four years ago, it is not to be despised.

To preface a bibliography by a bibliography would be a manifest work of supererogation. But a few words may be added here with respect to the Walmsley edition of 1817. In the sequence of illustrated volumes which followed upon the Bewick revival, it comes between the Ackermann's *Religious Emblems* of 1809 and the Bewick's *Fables of Æsop* of 1818. Bewick himself was a subscriber to the book, but he took no part in it, probably because he was fully occupied by his own *Fables*. The designs were wholly by John Thurston, who then enjoyed a monopoly in this way. Some of the most beautiful of the engravings were by John Thompson; others were by Bewick's pupils, Charlton Nesbit, Harvey, and White. The rest were by the two Branstons, by William Hughes, G. Thurston, Jun., and Mary Byfield, the clever lady who designed so many of the Chiswick Press decorations. The book was printed by John Johnson, of Clerkenwell, author of *Typographia*. According to Singer's preface to the edition of 1834, it was considered that in the common paper impressions of 1817 full justice had not been done to the engravings, and that in the edition of 1834, which was printed by Charles Whittingham under the superintendence of John Thompson, superior results had been obtained. But the judicious collector will probably continue to prefer the earlier issue, with its luxury of satin, and yellow Chinese paper, and coloured inks.

Your fellow Rowfanter,
AUSTIN DOBSON.

FEBRUARY, 1898.

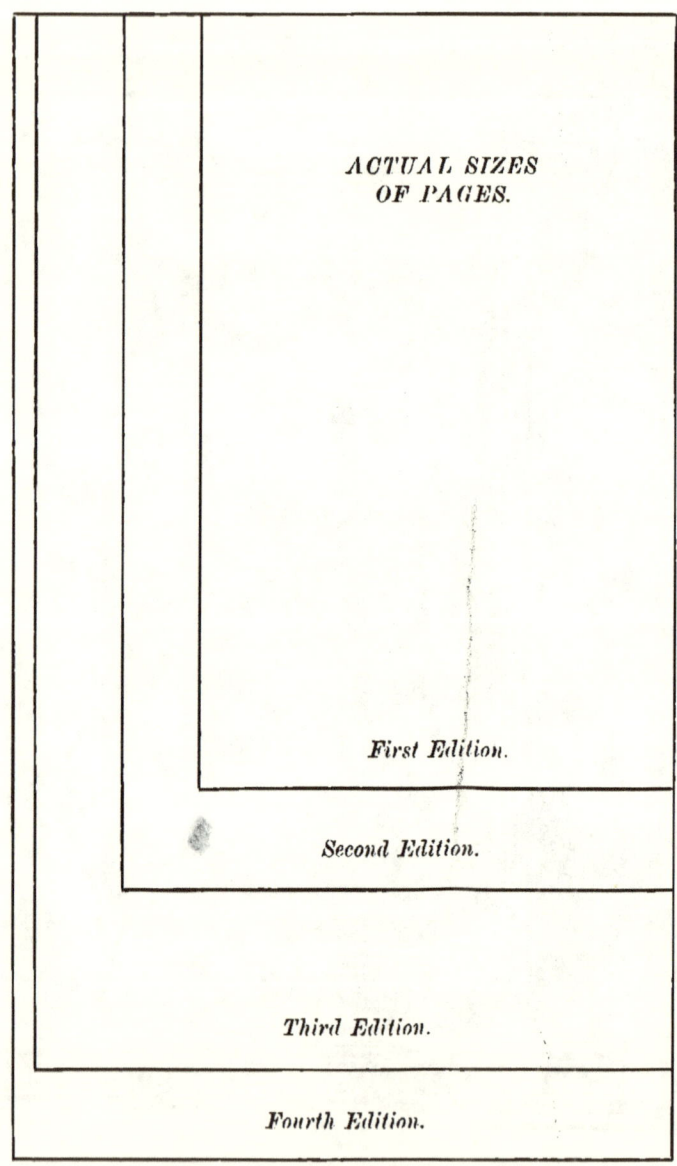

ACTUAL SIZES
OF PAGES.

First Edition.

Second Edition.

Third Edition.

Fourth Edition.

COMPARATIVE SIZES OF
THE FIRST FOUR EDITIONS.

PREFACE.

Diana's Temple at Ephesus being Burnt that Night Alexander was Born, One said, 'Twas no Wonder; for She was then a Gossiping at Pella: Which Tully commends as a witty Conceit, and Plutarch condemns as a witless Jest. Who then can expect an Essay of this Nature should (like the Manna) please every Palate? If it helps to set Youth a-Thinking; Th' End's Answered.——

(Preface from page 5, First Edition.)

CHARACTERS.

Antiquary.	Newsmonger.
Buffoon.	Opiniator.
Critick.	Projector.
Detractor.	Quack.
Envioso.	Rake.
Flatterer.	Swearer.
Gamester.	Traveller.
Hypocrite.	Usurer.
Impertinent.	Wiseman.
Knave.	Xantippe.
Lawyer.	a Youth.
Moroso.	Zany the Vintner.

These Characters being meerly intended to expose Vice and Folly; Let none Pretend to a Key, nor seek for another's Picture, lest he find his Own:

For, according to the Proverb, 'Tis Th' Application makes the Ass.

(First Edition, page 6.)

The Club:

Or, A

DIALOGUE

Between

Father and Son.

In Vino Veritas.

London,

Printed for the Author, and Sold by
S. Crouch at the Corner of *Pope's-
Head-Alley* in *Cornhill.* 1712.

SOMEWHAT OF THE BIBLIOGRAPHY OF "THE CLUB," FROM NOTES TAKEN AT A BOOK-SHOW HELD IN THE HOUSE OF THE ROWFANT CLUB.

WHILE there is no intention of going elaborately into the collation or other bibliographical description of these books, there *is* a desire to place in simple manner and definitely before the collector sufficient data to enable him to identify any copy of Puckle's Club which may be before him.

1 The Club: | Or, A | Dialogue | Between | Father and Son. | In Vino Veritas. | London, | Printed for the Author, and Sold by | S. Crouch at the Corner of Pope's- | Head-Alley in Cornhill, 1711.

Size, $2\frac{13}{16}$ x $4\frac{9}{16}$ inches.
Pages, 1 to 91, with 16 additional, "Dear Kinsman," etc.

NOTES. Page 1, title; 2, blank; 3, dedication; 4, blank; 5, "Preface" (see page 13); 6, "Characters" (see page 15); 7, "A | Dialogue | Between | Father and Son." And to page 91 the characters, "Antiquary" to "Zany"; then 16 pages, "Dear Kinsman" to "Finis." The beginning of the pagination is in top center of page within parentheses, (5), (6), (7), balance on upper corners. The heading is: "A Dialogue between Father and Son."

The present copy is bound in old calf, gilt corners, with a gilt border, and is not lettered on the back. All edges are gilt, and it is the smallest copy of the work.

This is the First Edition, of which there were two issues printed in the year 1711.

c

2 The Club: | Or, A | Dialogue | Between | Father and Son. | In Vino Veritas. | London: | Printed for the Author, | James Puckle.   1713.

Size, $3\frac{1}{4}$ x $5\frac{1}{2}$ inches.

Pages, 1 to 84 (including "Dear Kinsman," 67 to 84).

NOTES. Page 1, title; 2, dedication; 3, "Preface"; 4, "Characters"; 5, "A | Dialogue | Between | Father and Son." 3, 4, and 5 of pagination are in top center, inclosed in parentheses; 6 to 84, top corner of page, except 7, omitted.

This edition was entirely re-written with a view to smoothness; *e. g.*, the last sentence of "Character" is "Qui capit ille facit" instead of "'Tis Th' Application makes the Ass."

The binding of this copy is similar to that of the first edition, *q. v.*

This is the Second Edition.

The Club:

~~OR,~~ A
DIALOGUE

Between

Father and Son.

In Vino Veritas.

LONDON:
Printed for the Author,
James Puckle. 1713.

The Club.

IN A
DIALOGUE
Between
Father and Son.

In Vino Veritas.

The THIRD EDITION.

LONDON:
Printed for the Author,
1713.

3 The Club. | In A | Dialogue | Between | Father and Son. | In Vino Veritas. | The Third Edition. | London: | Printed for the Author, | 1713.

Size, $3\frac{4}{4}$ x $6\frac{3}{16}$ inches.

Pages, 1 to 70, with one page at the end ("General Titles in the Advice") unnumbered; 5, 6, and 7 in parentheses in top center of page, otherwise in upper corners.

NOTES. Page 0, portrait, facing to left, within elliptic frame with armorial design at foot; in panel below ellipse, "James Puckle, N. P. | J. B. Closterman pinx; G. Vertue Sculp."; page 1, title; page 2, blank; page 3, dedication, which differs from that shown on page 11, *q. v.*, in that "Merchants" becomes "Merchant", and "most Humble" is interpolated between "most Obliged" and "and most Obedient Servant"; page 4, "In Amicum suum Jacobum Puckle, Subsequentium Dialogorum Authorem; | Distichon. | Quanta Seges Rerum! parva patet Orbis in Urbe; | Et patet in Libro, Bibliotheca, Tuo. | H. Denne."; page 5, "Preface," same as second edition, with this addition:

"Go, Little Book, Show to the Fool his Face,
The Knave his Picture, and the Sot his Case:
Tell to each Youth, what is, and what's not, fit;
And Teach to such as want, Sobriety, and Wit.
J. P."

Page 6, "Characters," same as second edition.

This is the Third Edition, as lettered.

4 The Club. | In A | Dialogue | between | Father
and Son | In Vino Veritas | Cork: | Re-printed
from the Third Edition of a Lon- | don-Copy,
by Samuel Terry, in Cock-Pit-Lane | for John
Redwood, Bookseller, near the Ex- | change. |
Mdccxxi.

> Size, $3\frac{7}{8}$ x $5\frac{1}{4}$ inches.
> Pages, 1 to 70.

> NOTES. This edition is, as stated on the title-page, a re-
> print of the third regular edition. The "Distichon" on page
> 4, and "Preface," page 5, of third edition, are put upon one
> page, "Preface" being first, which includes "Go, Little
> Book," etc., the signature being "A2." The "Characters" are
> the same, even to the "N" in "ANtiquary." This is one of
> the scarce copies, seldom met with.

5 The Club. | Or, A | Grey-Cap, | For A | Green-Head, | In A | Dialogue | Between | Father and Son. 'In vino veritas. | The Fourth Edition, with Additions. | London, | Printed for Edward Symon, at the | Corner of Pope's-Head-Alley, Corn- | hill. 1723.

Size, 3⅞ x 6¼ inches.
Pages, (1) to (12), and 1 to 179.

NOTES. Page 0, portrait, re-engraved from third edition: the motto "Droit" is added in a ribbon below the armorial seal, within the panel is "James Puckle N. P." in script, and at bottom of plate "J. B. Closterman pinx. J. Cole Sculp."; page 1, title (the sub-title appears here for the first time); page (2), same as page 4, third edition; page (3), "A list of the Subscribers Names"; page (4), conclusion of list; page (5), dedication, beginning "Trade is the fountain | whence we draw our nourishment, dispensing that," etc., and ending on page (8). Notice that all three of the merchants are deceased at this time (1723). Page (9), "Preface," same as third edition, excepting the final signature "J. P.," which is omitted; pages 10 and 11, Index; page (12), "Characters," same as preceding edition. Page 1, "A | Dialogue | Between | Father and Son" to 94, then to page 148 "Maxims, Advice, and Cautions," etc.; page 149, "In All Your Glory | Memento Mori"; 150, blank; 151, "Preface"; 152, blank; 153, "Death" to 179. Pagination 3 to 12 in parentheses in top center of page, excepting 10 and 11, which are on top corners; pages 1 to 179, top corners. This edition is divided into verses from 1 to 1060, and is the last supervised by the author, who died the following year (1724). *See Steinman.*

This title-page, like that of the third edition, is calculated to make a purchaser of any book-lover. The reproduction shows the first arrangement of the sub-title (from Trenchfield, see item 26).

This is the Fourth Edition, and so lettered.

The Club.

OR, A

GREY-CAP,

FOR A

GREEN-HEAD,

IN A

DIALOGUE

Between

Father and Son.

In vino veritas.

The FOURTH EDITION, with Additions.

LONDON,

Printed for EDWARD SYMON, at the
Corner of *Pope's-Head-Alley*, *Cornhill*. 1723.

6 The Club: | Or, A Grey-Cap for a Green-Head. | Containing | Maxims, Advice and Cautions. | Being A Dialogue between a Father and Son. | In which is | Interspers'd the following Characters, Viz. |

Antiquary,	Newsmonger,
Buffoon,	Opiniater,
Critic,	Projector,
Detractor,	Quack,
Envioso,	Rake,
Flatterer,	Swearer,
Gamester,	Traveller,
Hypocrite,	Usurer,
Impertinent,	Wiseman,
Knave,	Xantippe,
Lawyer,	Youth,
Morose,	Zany the Vintner,

These characters being meerly intended, to ex-pose Vice and Folly; let none pretend to | a Key; nor seek for another's Picture, least | he find his own. For, | Qui capit ille facit. | In vino veritas. | The Fifth Edition, with Additions.

London: Printed for John King, at Sir | Walter
Raleigh's Head; And Thomas | King, at Shake-
spear's Head, both in ¦ Moorfields, near Little
Moorgate.

Size, $3\frac{3}{4}$ x $6\frac{3}{8}$ inches.
Pages, same as fourth edition.

NOTES. Distich on reverse of title-page omitted.
This copy is undoubtedly made from a remainder of fourth
edition by changing title-page, etc.
Lettered, "Fifth Edition, with Additions," but plainly a
spurious edition.

7 The Club: | etc.; being same as preceding, except type, the putting of a comma after "Advice," "Opiniater" spelled "Opiniator," and the imprint, which is as follows: London, | Printed for Edward Symon, against the Royal | Exchange in Cornhill.   M.dcc.xxxiii.

Size, $3\frac{11}{16}$ x $6\frac{1}{4}$ inches.
Pages, same as fourth edition.

NOTES. Spurious; same as preceding item, except as above noted.   (See reproduction of title-page.)

The C L U B:

OR, A
Grey-Cap for a *Green-Head.*

CONTAINING
Maxims, Advice, *and* Cautions.

BEING A
DIALOGUE between a *Father* and *Son.*

In which is
Interfpers'd the following Characters,

VIZ.

Antiquary,	Newfmonger,
Buffoon,	Opiniator,
Critic,	Projector,
Detractor,	Quack,
Enviofo,	Rake,
Flatterer,	Swearer,
Gamefter,	Traveller,
Hypocrite,	Ufurer,
Impertinent,	Wifeman,
Knave,	Xantippe,
Lawyer,	Youth,
Morofe,	Zany *the Vintner.*

Thefe Characters being meerly intended, to
expofe Vice and Folly; let none pretend to
a Key; nor feek for another's Picture, leaft
he find his own. For,

Qui capit ille facit.

In vino veritas.

The FIFTH EDITION, with Additions.

LONDON,
Printed for EDWARD SYMON, *againft the* Royal
Exchange *in* Cornhill. M.DCC.XXXIII.

8 The Club: | Or, A Grey-Cap for a Green Head. | Containing | Maxims, Advice, and Cautions. | Being A | Dialogue between a Father and Son. | In which is | Interspers'd the following Characters, | Viz. |

Antiquary,	Newsmonger,
Buffoon,	Opiniator,
Critic,	Projector,
Detractor,	Quack,
Envioso,	Rake,
Flatterer,	Swearer,
Gamester,	Traveller,
Hypocrite,	Usurer,
Impertinent,	Wiseman,
Knave,	Xantippe,
Lawyer,	Youth,
Morose,	Zany the Vintner.

These Characters being merely intended, to expose Vice | and Folly; let none pretend to a Key; nor seek for | another's Picture, lest he find his own. For, | Qui capit ille facit. | In vino veritas. The Sixth Edition, with Additions. | Dublin: |

Printed by S. Powell, | For William Heatly, at the
Bible and Dove in | College-green, Mdccxxxvii.

Size, $3\frac{7}{8} \times 6\frac{1}{2}$ inches.
Pages, 20 and 1 to 188. Index, 5 additional.

NOTES. Page 0, portrait by Closterman, once more re-engraved. This time facing to the right with names of artists
omitted. Page 1, title, very similar to the spurious fifth edition; 2, blank; 3, "Dedication," same as preceding item with
headpiece, birds within scrolls, Ceres distributing fruits to
two cupids; pages 4, 5, and 6, continuation of dedication; 7,
"Preface"; 8, "Characters"; 9, the subscribers' names; headpiece, a cock within floriated scrollwork; 9 to 19, list of names
continued; 20, blank. Pages 1 to 101, "A Dialogue | Between |
Father and Son"; headpiece, hawks and scrolls; then 101 to
188, "Maxims," etc., and "Death." Following which are five
pages "Index" and two pages "Catalogue," "Books printed
for and sold by William Heatly, Bookseller," etc. The entire
work is divided into 1060 verses or paragraphs, numbered
consecutively. A most interesting copy.

Lettered, "Sixth Edition, with Additions."

9 The Club: | etc. Same as the preceding, except-
ing, "The Seventh Edition, with Additions. |
Dublin: | Printed for Peter Wilson, Bookseller, at
Gay's-head, | near Fowns's-street, in Dame-street.
Mdccxliii.

> Size, $3\frac{5}{8}$ x $6\frac{1}{4}$ inches.
> Pages, same as preceding item.
>
> NOTES. No portrait. Catalogue at end omitted.
> Although lettered "Seventh Edition," this is undoubtedly
> another remainder. Nothing but the title-page was changed
> from the edition of 1737, which, like the unfortunate fourth
> edition, seems to have been almost unsalable.

10 The Club: | Or, A | Grey Cap | For A | Green Head; | In A | Dialogue | Between | Father and Son. | In vino veritas. | The Fifth Edition. Edinburgh: | Printed by Tho. and Wal. Ruddimans, and sold by | the Booksellers in Town. 1756.

Size, $3\frac{1}{4}$ x $5\frac{3}{4}$.
Pages, i–viii, and 1 to 124.

NOTES. Page i, title; ii, "Distich"; iii–vi, "Dedication"; vii, "Preface"; viii, "Characters"; all unnumbered, excepting iv and v, within brackets; 1 to 74, "A | Dialogue | Between | Father and Son"; 74 to 96, Wiseman's letter, "Dear Kinsman," etc.; 97, "In all your Glory Memento Mori"; 98, "Preface"; 99 to 124, "Death."

This is a beautiful little book, lettered "Fifth Edition." (Only one copy in this collection, and presumably rare.)

The Club:

OR, A

GREY CAP

FOR A

GREEN HEAD;

IN A

DIALOGUE

BETWEEN

FATHER AND SON.

IN VINO VERITAS.

PHILADELPHIA:
PRINTED BY FRANCIS BAILEY, AT YORICK'S
HEAD, N°. 116, HIGH-STREET.
M,DCC,XCV.

11   The Club: | Or, A | Grey Cap | For A | Green Head; | In A | Dialogue | Between | Father and Son. | In Vino Veritas. | Philadelphia: | Printed by Francis Bailey, at Yorick's | Head, No. 116, High-street. | M,dcc,xcv.

> Size, 3¼x6 inches, uncut.
> Pages, 1 to 198.

> NOTES. Pages 120 to 155, "Dear Kinsman"; 156, blank; 157, "In All Your Glory | Memento Mori"; 159, "Preface"; 160, "Death" to "Finis"; i, ii, iii, vi, vii, viii, and ix unnumbered; iv, v, in parentheses, top center of page; 10 to 198 top corner of page; page 1, title; ii, blank; iii to (v), "To | Micajah Perry, | and | Thomas Lane, Esquires, | and | Mr. Richard Perry"; vi, blank; vii, "Preface"; viii, "Characters"; ix, "A | Dialogue | Between | Father and Son."
>
> This is an interesting edition, and very rare. The above copy is as new. It is printed on Dutch paper. The blank flyleaves are of different and coarser paper. The binding is gray boards with vellum back. The bottoms of leaves are very irregular, sometimes showing as much as one inch difference in margins. It is beautifully printed. This is the first American edition. It collates with the edition of 1756 (item 10, *q. r.*).
>
> This copy has the library ticket of Walter Cresson, and is first noted in "XVIIIth Century Vignettes," 1896.

12 ❧ The Club; | In | A Dialogue | Between | Father
And Son. | 1817. (Monogram E. W. in wreath of
laurel.)

Size, 7¼ x 10¾ inches, uncut.

Pages, 000000 to 0, unnumbered; i–xviii; 1–96; i, xi to
xviii, unnumbered, otherwise numbers in panels of border, top center of page.

NOTES. Page 000000, "This Edition | of | Puckle's Club | is
Printed for the Proprietor, | By John Johnson: | and sold
by | Longman, Hurst, Rees, Orme and Brown, | Paternoster
Row; | J. Major, Skinner Street; | John and Arthur Arch,
Cornhill; | and Robert Triphook, | Old Bond Street; | Lon-
don. | Mdcccxvii." 00000, "The Impression of this Edi-
tion | is as follows: | Large paper (Imperial) Two Hundred. |
Small Paper (Royal) Five Hundred. | Chinese Paper (White)
Eighteen. | Chinese Paper (Yellow) Seven. Satin (Mounted
on Imperial) Seven. | Various Colours (Printed On One Side)
One. | Blue, One. Yellow, One." Page 0000, blank; 000, por-
trait (facing to left) in the fourth state of the plate: "James
Puckle Esqr. | Engraved for this Edition of the Club | by
T. Bragg. | From an original Portrait | by Vertue. | E. W.
Oct. 1817." 00, title, scene of drunken brawl, fourteen
characters in panel at top within intricately engraved design by John Thompson after Thurston; 0, blank. Pages
i to iv, "To The Reader"; v to ix, "List of Subscribers";
x, ❧; xi, "The Club: | In A | Dialogue | Between | Father
and Son. In Vino Veritas. London: Printed for the
Author, James Puckle. 1711," printed in red and black;
xii, blank; xiii, "To Micajah Perry, Esq. | And | The grate-
ful Memory | of | Thomas Lane, Esq. | Deceased; and to |
Mr. Richard Perry, of London; Merchants: | The follow-

ing | Dialogue, | As | A Pepper-Corn Acknowledgment, | Is Humbly | Dedicated, | By | Their Most Obliged, | And | Most Obedient Servant, | James Puckle." Page 96, "London: Imprinted by J. Johnson, | St. James's Street, | Clerkenwell. | Mdcccxvii." Pages i to xviii printed within red borders, the following pages within black borders. The original binding is gray boards; on front cover appears, "Puckle's | Club | 1817" in panel of double rules. Inside of front cover is the subscription ticket: "Subscriber's Copy. | Small Paper. | Puckle's Club. | New Edition | No—". Five hundred of this size were printed, this copy being No. 239.

The Club;

IN

A DIALOGUE

BETWEEN

FATHER AND SON.

1817

13 The same, uncut, and on better paper, the original binding being red silk with gold border similar to satin copy (item 17, *q. v.*).

The portrait is in the second state of the plate, viz: "T Bragg Sculpt" to right of vignette, and "*James Puckle Esqr.* | E. W. Oct. 1817."

A curious variation seldom seen. Of more than thirty of these portraits examined, this was the only one in this state.

14 The Club; | In | A Dialogue | Between | Father and Son. | 1817. (Monogram E. W. within laurel wreath below.)

Size, 7⅝ x 10¾ inches, uncut.
Pages, same as item 12.

NOTES. This is the Large Paper (Imperial) edition. The portrait is in the third state of the plate, the word "Proof" having been added at right hand lower corner. The engravings are on India paper, mounted, excepting portrait, title-page, and tail-pieces. The original binding is gray boards, with white vellum back, all plain. It was limited to 200 copies, this copy being No. 44. There are twenty-two copies of this edition in this collection, many being prized for their contemporary bindings, autographs, or ex-libris.

15 The Club; | In | A Dialogue | Between | Father and Son. | 1817. (With monogram, etc.)

Size, 7½ x 10¾ inches, uncut.
Pages, mounted on one side of 116 leaves.

NOTES. This is the variant advertised as upon "White Chinese Paper, Mounted on One Side only." In addition to the ordinary ruling there is printed on the edge of the Chinese paper a border of Greek fret one-eighth of an inch wide — the whole within a beautiful framework of vine and leaves, with small corners of a four-leaved flower. The portrait is in the *first state of the plate*, an artist's proof before all letters. The portrait in the first state is very uncommon; some of the "uniques" do not carry it.

It is a most sumptuous and noble book. The present copy is bound in red crushed levant morocco, without a binder's ticket or mark. Eighteen copies were made. They were unnumbered.

16 The Club; | etc. 1817. Same as item 12.

Everything said in praise of the preceding book may be said of this. It is on yellow paper. In the present copy a striking ticket is printed as follows, "Puckle's Club. | 1817." and pasted on fly-leaf. Of this sort only seven copies were made, unnumbered. See reproduction of binding opposite, the tooling being copied from ornaments used in the book.

17 The Club; | etc. 1817.

Size, $7\frac{1}{8}$ x $10\frac{3}{16}$.
Pages, 116 leaves.

NOTES. This is one of the most beautiful works of its
kind. It is printed on satin mounted on one side of the leaf
only. The satin is pasted on inside of the regular border,
the joint being hidden by a broad gold line; this line is inside of an elaborate tooled design of conventionalized lilies,
while at the corner, projecting one-half inch beyond the line,
is the Greek honeysuckle. All the tooled work is in pure
gold, applied to the sheet. The tooling is superbly done by
a master workman. The present copy is absolutely spotless
and without fault. No description can do it justice. On
this copy all edges are gilt, and it is sumptuously bound.
The portrait, however, is of the third state of the plate as
previously described. Of this book only seven copies were
made. They were unnumbered.

18 The Club; | etc. 1817.

This copy is practically the same as the foregoing, but
seems to have been a trifle taller. It is printed in bluish-
green ink, and is not so attractive to look upon as some
of the foregoing. The binding is old calf, ornamented in
straight lines. It is unique, only one copy having been
made.

James Puckle. N° 1°

19 The Club; | etc. 1817.

Size, 6 x 9¼ inches. Gilt edges.
Pages, same as item 12, *q. v.*

NOTES. This copy has been made up so as to take the proofs of all engravings mounted on the ordinary page, within the regulation borders, the duplicates (proofs) being *colored by hand.* The portrait is in the fourth state, which must have been an oversight. The ex-libris of "William Crawford. | Lakelands. | Cork" is inside front cover. Probably unique in this state.

20 The Club; | etc. 1817.

Size, $7\frac{5}{16}$ x $10\frac{13}{16}$ inches. Top edges gilt.
Pages, same as item 12, *q. v.*

NOTES. This is undoubtedly a copy of the imperial octavo edition with this variation: All the engravings, including the portrait, are printed on a curious rice paper, of a bright orange color. The portrait is of the third state of the plate, and mounted in a small panel instead of filling the page. Probably unique in this form.

The book is very tall, the paper of a better and thinner quality than the regular. A beautiful example of fine bookmaking, and, like the preceding item, unknown in duplicate to the present owner of the collection. There is no authority for these last two books in the list on page 00000, item 12.

Bound by Bedford; see reproduction opposite. Ex-libris, Mervyn Marshall.

21 The Club; | Or, | A Gray Cap For A Green Head. | A Dialogue | Between A Father And Son. | By James Puckle. | (Portrait.) | Chiswick Press: | Printed By C. Whittingham. | Sold By Charles Tilt, Fleet Street, London: | And N. Hailes, Piccadilly.   M dccc xxxiv.

Size, 4⁵⁄₁₆ x 6¾ inches, uncut.

Pages, i to xx and 1 to 128; catalogue, etc., 1 to 24.

NOTES. Pages i–v, xiii–xv, xvii–xx, 1 and 1–2, all inclusive, unnumbered. Page i, engraving of "Brawl" from title-page 1817; ii, title; iii, blank; iv to xii, "The | Editor's Preface, [By "S. W. S.," Mr. S. W. Singer, the Shakespearean scholar,] | Mickleham, July 12, 1833"; xiii, reproduction of title-page of "1733." This is nothing like it, but very like Edinburgh, 1756. A similar error is noted on page vii, where 1733 is quoted when 1723 is undoubtedly meant. Again, Mr. Singer speaks of James Puckle being alive to supervise a Fifth Edition in 1733; Puckle died in 1724. See "XVIIIth Century Vignettes," 1896. xiv, blank; xv–xvi, "Dedication" (ed. 1733); xvii, "The | Author's Preface"; xviii, tail-piece to Opiniator; xix, "Characters"; xx, "Go, little book," etc.; 1 to 124, "The Club; or, | A Gray Cap for a Green Head"; 125 to 128, "Description of the cuts; designed and drawn by Mr. Thurston"; 1 to 24, "Catalogue | of | Embellished Books," etc. The cuts are from the original blocks now in the possession of Messrs. George Bell & Sons, London.

Charles Whittingham, S. W. Singer, and Rev. John Mitford thought that justice was not done to the beautiful work of Thurston in the edition of 1817, the letter-press, in their

THE CLUB;

OR,

A GRAY CAP FOR A GREEN HEAD.

A DIALOGUE
BETWEEN A FATHER AND SON.

By JAMES PUCKLE.

𝕮𝖍𝖎𝖘𝖜𝖎𝖈𝖐 𝕻𝖗𝖊𝖘𝖘:

PRINTED BY C. WHITTINGHAM.
SOLD BY CHARLES TILT, FLEET STREET, LONDON;
AND N. HAILES, PICCADILLY.

M DCCC XXXIV.

opinion, being faulty. The proposition was made to Whittingham to make a perfect book, that would be a credit to the Chiswick Press, and the result is a gratifying exhibit of the capabilities of that celebrated printing-shop. The engravings have been enumerated and described elsewhere, but the appendix is interesting also for its illustrations, though intended only for an advertisement. They are as follows: Page 1, Falstaff surrounded by his coterie; 3, The four Virgins (Northcote's Fables); 4, The Ass and the Dog; 5, Portrait; 6, Falstaff at the Death of Hotspur; 7, Frontispiece; 9, Portrait; 10, Garden Scene; 11, The Chittah, or Hunting Leopard; 12, The Third Age of Man, and The Favorite of the Harem; 13, Selborne; 14, Bird, etc.; 15, Detractor; 16, The House in which Shakespeare was Born; 17, Frontispiece to Second Edition, Singer's Shakespeare; 19, King Lear; 20, Portraits of Johnson, and "Cupid Caged"; 21, War scene; 22, From Tom Jones; 23, Two illustrations from new books. All from publications of the Chiswick Press.

There seems to have been no uniformity in the original bindings of "The Club"; of 27 copies of this edition, item 21, in this collection, many of which are ment, only three are alike in design, and they differ in color—brown, red, and blue cloth, stamped with some geometric design, predominating. The book as a whole is satisfactory, though not by any means the best thing done by Charles Whittingham.

As previously noted, a great deal of the information in Mr. Singer's Preface is either incorrect or misleading; *e. g.*, on page 8 the statement is made that "His [Puckle's] portrait, by Closterman, engraved by Cole, was first prefixed to an edition in 1723, and twice again re-engraved by Vertue for subsequent impressions." The 1813 (third) edition first had the Closterman portrait; Vertue did not engrave subsequent portraits, but the *first*. J. Cole made the portrait in the edition of 1723.

The edition of 1834 is common, and though not so pleasing to a book-lover as the third edition (1713), nor so satisfying to the collector as one of the large copies of 1817, the ordinary reader will do well, having acquired it, to rest content.

22 The Club; | etc.

Size, $4\frac{3}{8}$ x $6\frac{3}{4}$ inches, uncut.
Pages, same as preceding item.

NOTES. This is the same edition on cheap paper. The only difference is that on title-page after "Sold by Charles Tilt, Fleet Street, London" appears, "And William Jackson, New York."

23 The Club; | etc.

Size, 4 x $6\frac{1}{2}$ inches.
Pages, same as preceding item.

NOTES. This is a copy of the 1834 edition on white Chinese paper. It is less than one-fourth inch in thickness, and is complete, including Chiswick Press advertisements. All edges are gilt.

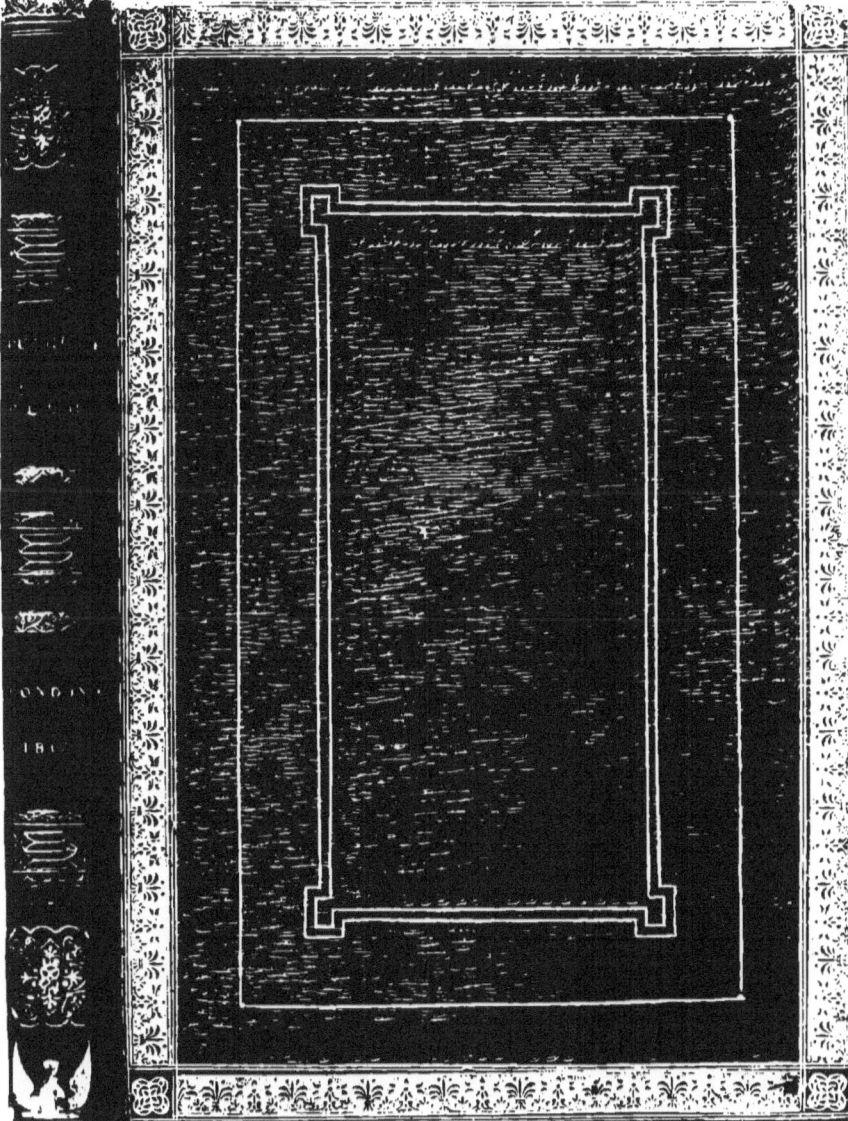

THE CLUB

OR

A GRAY CAP FOR A GREEN HEAD

A DIALOGUE

BETWEEN A FATHER AND SON

BY

JAMES PUCKLE, N.P.

GLASGOW
DAVID BRYCE AND SON
1890

24 The Club ' Or ' A Gray Cap For A Green Head | A Dialogue | Between A Father And Son | By | James Puckle, N. P. | (Portrait.) | Glasgow | David Bryce And Son   1890

Size, $3\frac{7}{16}$ x $5\frac{1}{4}$ inches, uncut.

Pages, 1 to 160—1 to 3 unnumbered; 4 to 9 center of bottom of page, excepting 5 and 6 unnumbered; 10 to 160 top corner of page.

NOTES. Page 1, "The Club | Or | A Gray Cap For A Green Head"; 2, "Brawl"; 3, title; 4, "Reprinted from the Edition of 1833"; 5, reproduction of title-page of Fourth Edition (1723); 6, blank; 7, "The | Author's Preface"; 8, "Characters"; 9 to 17, "The | Editor's Preface" (1833); 18, "Go, little book," etc.; 19 to 155, "The Club; | Or, | A Gray Cap For A Green Head"; 156 to 160, "Description of the Cuts." Every page printed within red border. The Thurston cuts are used in the form of very poor reproductions much reduced in size. The original binding is undressed sheep, natural, tied with purple ribbon. Stamped on the outside is the following: "The Club. | Or, A | Grey-Cap, | For A Green-Head, | In A | Dialogue | Between | Father and Son."

25 The Club | etc.

Size, same as preceding.
Pages, same as preceding.

NOTES. This is the same book, excepting in place of "Glasgow | David Bryce and Son | 1890" is "New York | Frederick A. Stokes and Brother," n. d.

APPENDIX.

A LARGE amount of material is at hand bearing directly or indirectly on Puckle's "Club," some of which might properly be included, while to use a great deal would be filling space unnecessarily. It has seemed expedient, however, to note a few items which appear to be of considerable interest.

26 A | Cap | Of | Gray Hairs | For A | Green Head: etc. | By Caleb Trenchfield, Gent. | London: | 1710. (See reproduction.)

> Size, 4¼ x 6½ inches.
> Pages, 8 unnumbered, then 1 to 149 (page 3 unnumbered).
>
> NOTES. Puckle has been accused of appropriating a part of this title for his sub-title in the edition of 1723. A glance at this 1710 "Trenchfield" will show this to be true.

A

C A P

OF

Gray Hairs

FOR A

GREEN HEAD:

OR, THE

FATHERS COUNSEL

TO HIS

S O N,

An Apprentice in *LONDON*.

Containing wholesome Instructions for the Mauagement of a Mans whole LIFE.

The Fifth Edition.

With Additions of Precepts adapted to each Chapter.

By *CALEB TRENCHFIELD*, Gent.

LONDON:
Printed for *A. Bettesworth,* at the *Red Lyon* on *London-Bridge.* 1710.

27 Illustrations | To | Puckle's Club: | ☙ | ☙ | Printed
(For The Proprietor) In Colours, | From The Origi-
nal Blocks, | And Limited To One Hundred Im-
pressions. | 1820.

Size, $6\frac{3}{4} \times 9\frac{3}{10}$ inches, uncut.
Pages, 27 leaves. Unnumbered.

NOTES. Leaf 1, title; 2, "The Proprietor of the late | Edi-
tion of Puckle's Club, has | been at much additional expense |
in order to present the principal | Embellishments, executed
for that | Work, in their present form, which being almost
entirely novel in this | Country, | he trusts they cannot | fail
to interest the lovers of the | Fine Arts, the prosperity of
which | he is ardently desirous to promote"; 3, Description
of the Engravings; 4 to 27 inclusive, proofs of engravings,
"Antiquary" to "Zany," India paper, mounted, with title
beneath in capitals.   Originally bound in gray boards, with
"Illustrations | To | Puckle's Club. | Printed In Colours" in-
side panel on first cover.

One hundred copies made.   Unnumbered.

ILLUSTRATIONS
TO
PUCKLE'S CLUB:

PRINTED (FOR THE PROPRIETOR) IN COLOURS,
FROM THE ORIGINAL BLOCKS,
AND LIMITED TO ONE HUNDRED IMPRESSIONS.

1820.

England's Intereſt:

OR,

A Brief Diſcourſe

OF THE

Royal Fiſhery.

IN

A Letter to a Friend.

The Second Edition.

LONDON:

Printed by *J. Southby*, at the *Har-
row* in *Cornhill.* 1 6 9 6.

28 England's Interest: | Or, | A Brief Discourse | Of
The | Royal Fishery. | In | A Letter to a Friend. |
etc.

> Size, $4\frac{1}{5}$x$6\frac{1}{2}$ inches, uncut.
> Pages, 2 unnumbered, then 1 to 38.
>
> NOTES. In the introduction to this Bibliography mention
> is made of two other books by James Puckle. Space is taken
> here to show somewhat of his first book, though not of course
> properly admitted. There are interesting variations of this
> book.

29 Printers' Proofs | From | Puckle's Club.

> Size, 7x$10\frac{3}{16}$ inches, gilt edges.
> Pages, 34 leaves.
>
> NOTES. This is a book made up of the printers' proofs of
> all the engravings in 1817 edition Puckle's Club, (some dupli-
> cates,) including seven (Walmsley mentions only four) which
> were refused because of mechanical or artistic defects and
> therefore not to be seen in the book.
>
> These include proofs from tint-blocks also, *separate from
> the cuts.*
>
> An interesting item, probably unique.

30 The Author | Of | "The Club" | Identified. | By | G. Steinman Steinman, Esq., F. S. A. | Printed for private Circulation. | 1872.

Size, $4\frac{3}{4} \times 7\frac{3}{8}$ inches, uncut.
Pages, 20.

NOTES. To know Puckle is to think of Steinman, whose rare pamphlet is herewith noted. This copy is in the original yellow paper covers, and bears on the flyleaf Mr. Steinman's autograph inscription, "The R^t Hn^{ble} Earl Stanhope, F. S. A. &c. | with the author's best Comp^s & regards | 8th July 1872." It is a valuable item in connection with "The Club," and as only about twenty were printed for private circulation, it is necessarily scarce.

31 No Title.

Size, $4\frac{7}{8} \times 9\frac{1}{4}$ inches, gilt edges.
Pages, 30 leaves.

NOTES. This is J. Thompson's own book of proofs of his work, including those engraved by him for "The Club." Beautifully bound in old green morocco, neatly tooled, and lettered on back as follows: "Engravings | By | Thompson | J. T." (Monogram.) Unique.
See reproduction of binding on page 66.

THE AUTHOR

OF

"THE CLUB"

IDENTIFIED.

BY

G. STEINMAN STEINMAN, ESQ., F.S.A.

Printed for private Circulation.
1872.

FROM WALMSLEY'S PREFACE TO 1817 EDITION PUCKLE'S CLUB.

The present Edition is indebted to the able pencil of Mr. Thurston for the Designs with which it is illustrated; and it is presumed that the man of taste, as well as the artist, will admit that each tells the story of its peculiar subject with appropriate expression. And were it necessary to dwell on the merits of the Author, it would of itself be no mean praise, that in the hands of a masterly Designer it should have become the vehicle of so fine a series of humorous and characteristic prints. With respect to the execution of the Cuts by the several Engravers, it may be allowable here to remark, that the labour of producing a good engraving on wood is more considerable, and requires more of art, than has generally been supposed; and it is but justice to those who have been employed in this part of the Work, to inform the Reader, that every line of the drawing is marked out upon the block by the Designer, exactly as it appears upon the paper; from this delineation it is the province of the Engraver to cut out a perfect and well-wrought resemblance; to effect which, great ability is requisite, as the least deviation is irremediable, especially when what is technically termed cross-hatching occurs, as is fully exemplified in the decoration of this volume. To give a slight idea of the difficulty of such operation, it is only necessary to observe, that every minute interstice of white is cut out with the graver from between every mark of the Designer's pencil. In consequence of this indispensable nicety, the Proprietor, sparing no expense to present the Work as faultless as possible has thrown aside four beautiful Designs, which were rendered useless by such deviation; and the same designs have been retraced on new blocks.

The Portrait prefixed has been most accurately copied by T. Bragg, a pupil of the present celebrated Mr. Sharp, from an original engraving by Vertue, after a painting by J. B. Closterman, and its genuineness is authenticated by the Earl of Orford, in his "Catalogue of Engravers," in which he particularizes the Original.

PORTRAITS.

Although many of the portraits have been described in previous items, it might be well to collate them here in one place for reference: First, the original painting by Closterman; after that the following: Vertue, item 3; J. Cole, item 5; unknown engraver, item 7; T. Bragg, four states, items 15, 13, 14, and 12; unknown, item 8; unknown artist, a large drawing in the possession of the owner of this collection of "Puckles"; small cut used in Glasgow edition (1890); etching used in 1896 on an invitation to a Rowfant Club exhibition, and again in the prospectus of this bibliography; finally, the etching by T. Johnson, frontispiece to this book.

DESCRIPTION OF THE CUTS,

With the names of the engravers, the whole designed and drawn by Mr. Thurston.

[From 1817 Edition.]

First Letters to Advertisement and Dialogue, and first T.P. [Tail-Piece] R. Branston.

Antiquary . . attempting to decypher the inscription on an old rusty coin or medal. J. Thompson. T.P., W. Hughes.

Buffoon . . . endeavoring, by his anticks and grimaces to "out-fool" the company. H. White. T.P., ditto.

Critic . . . with his face turned away to denote his desire of concealment; but the Artist has reflected it in the glass, to shew the mind that actuates him. R. Branston. T.P., R. Branston, Jun.

Detractor . . instilling suspicion into the mind of a credulous old man, by ill-natured surmises respecting the two persons walking in the adjoining garden. J. Thompson. T.P., H. White.

Envioso . . brooding over the malevolence of his heart in a re-tired cave, and turning with envious hate from the mirthful sports of a group of happy rustics. R. Branston. T.P., J. Thompson.

Flatterer . . paying court to a great man. J. Thompson. T.P., W. Hughes.

Gamester . . having ruined his man, gathers up his spoils with a cold-hearted indifference. W. Hughes. T.P., R. Branston, Jun.

Hypocrite . having thrown off the mask of loyalty in his cups, is aiming a side blow at Church and State, by his attacks upon a Prime Minister. J. Thompson. T.P., H. White.

Impertinent . detains a merchant from his appointment with officious and frivolous pretences. J. Thompson. T.P., H. White.

Knave . . . The doors shut upon rejected Stock Jobbers. W. Hughes. T.P., J. Thompson.

Lawyer . . a limb of the law bribing a witness. R. Branston. T.P., W. Hughes.

Moroso . . a repulsive churl, whom even his domestics fear to approach. J. Thompson. T.P., R. Branston, Jun.

Newsmonger. so completely absorbed in his own political impressions and sagacious remarks, that he does not perceive he has read his auditor asleep. J. Thompson. T.P., W. Hughes.

Opiniator . . one proud of his ancestry, and having tired all his friends with his pedigree, &c., is reduced to the necessity of making an auditor of his lackey. J. Thompson. T.P., R. Branston, Jun.

Projector . . contemplating a castle in the air. W. Hughes.

Quack . . . so deeply deliberating upon a patient's case, that he does not notice the nurse who has brought a monkey for advice. C. Nesbit. T.P., R. Branston.

Rake . . . endeavouring to drown the reflection of his overnight's debauch, and new string his shaken nerves by fresh stimulants. Miss Byfield.

Swearer . . driving a good old man out of the room by his shocking oaths, and checked by the simple reproof of his affrighted grandchild, who puts her hand upon his lips. J. Thompson, T.P., G. Thurston, Jun., first attempt.

Traveller . . a travelled fop ridiculing to his foreign lackey the homely welcome of his affectionate Parents. H. White. T.P., J. Thompson.

Usurer. . . poring over his annuity deeds and mortgages, his iron chests and bags filled with the prey of his avarice. J. Thompson. T.P., H. White.

Wiseman . . an anxious father instructing the minds, and regulating the hearts of his children. J. Thompson.

Xantippe . . a scolding wife, bringing home a drunken husband from his Club. J. Thompson. T.P., W. Harvey, a pupil of T. Bewick.

Youth . . an idle, dissipated young man of fashion, killing time by playing with his cat. J. Thompson. T.P., R. Branston, Jun.

Zany . . a sot, closing the scene in his cellar. C. Nesbit.

Tail Piece . page 95. R. Branston.

The Club . . in full assembly: design on the Title Page explained by the text, page 69. J. Thompson.

"*In amicum suum* JACOBUM PUCKLE,
subsequentium Dialogorum Authorem :
Distichon.
Quanta seges rerum! parvâ patet
orbis in urbe; et patet in libro,
Bibliotheca, tuo."

THE MARION PRESS, JAMAICA, QUEENSBOROUGH, NEW-YORK.